Jazzy's Bitch

A Thriller Series by

Krystol

Krystol

Jazzy's Bitch

Jazzy's Bitch A Thriller Series

This is a work of fiction. The events and characters described here and imaginary and are not intended to refer to specific places or living persons.

 Published by: Krystol Diggs Publishing

Written by: Krystol

Edited by: Jamila E. Gomez

Cover Design by: Junnita Jackson

Krystol

Dedication

This story is dedicated to all of my fans. Without you my work wouldn't be possible. I appreciate the love and support that you have shown me through out my writing career. I hope that I continue to please you with my stories!

Acknowledgements

I just want to first thank God for giving me the gift of life and writing.

To my family and friends, I thank you for always having my back and being there when I needed you too.

To my publicist Shawnda Hamilton, Thank you so much for all that you do. We work hard, but you work harder. Much love to you.

To my author friends, there are too many to name! Thank you for always listening about being in this writing game, much appreciated.

Readers: I hope that you enjoy my short story series! Please leave a review!

Check me out and show love:

Website: www.writingbykrystol.com

Twitter: @Krystol1,@jazzybitch24

Krystol

Fanpage: www.facebook.com/writingbykrystol

**Everything That Glitters Isn't
Gold**

"Jazzy, please leave me alone. I'm tired of being in this business. I want out!" I was screaming at the top of my lungs. My eyebrow rose in fear as I thought that he was going to hit me again for speaking my mind.

"Didn't I tell you that you are to be seen and not heard?" he shouted back at me. This time, he was in my face. The smell of his breath almost had me huddled over because it was indeed tart. I thought to myself, *how did I get here?* I graduated college at the top of my class, and yet, I'm selling my body and giving the money to another man. Not a good look! Who would have thought that I'd be where I am today, with me being as intelligent as I am? My pimp's name was Jazon, aka "Jazzy." He had been a pimp for quite some time, but I didn't know it when I first met him. He decided to show me his true colors after the fact. I remember the day like it was yesterday.

I was walking on Madison Street in Delaware, where I used to live. I had just graduated college the week before. I noticed a guy standing on the corner looking at me while I was waiting for the bus. Jazzy was fine as all outdoors. He had a 6'2 frame with brown caramel skin and the nicest smile that would light up a room. I was definitely interested just from his looks alone. I had been single for about a year and it was time to get back into the game. Little did I know I should have kept walking that day. My curiosity had got the best of me.

"How you doin', lil' mama?"

"Lil' mama?" He had a southern accent that I couldn't quite wrap my finger around. I was pleasant and kind because I could tell that he wasn't from here.

"Hi, how are you?"

"I'm good!"

"Where are you from?" I asked him.

"I'm from Atlanta."

"I see."

"What's your name?"

"My name is Jazon, but my peoples call me Jazzy, shawty."

"Well, Jazzy, I'm Karmen."

We both stood there observing each other like we were superstars excited to see one another. I knew I looked sexy. I stood 5'8 with a butterscotch complexion, tiny waist, and big backside someone could sit a wine glass on. My breasts weren't so small either.

"So, lil' mama where you headed?"

"The Mall."

"Want a ride there?" I knew I was supposed to say no, but Jazzy had me hooked. There was no stopping me. The day was young, and I hoped the night would be even better.

"Okay."

"Cool...my ride is the Silver BMW across the street."

"Okay."

I noticed Jazzy checking me out as I was going across the street. What was weird to me was that he was still standing on the corner until a young boy came gave him some money. Then he came to the car. I thought to myself, *Wow, he's a trap boy.*

When he got into the car, I was ready to decline the ride because I didn't hang with drug dealers. Before I could say anything, he began to speak.

"No, lil' mama. I don't sell drugs but I do have people working for me."

"You think that makes it any better?"

"No, but I can take care of you."

He pulled out six wads of money rolled up in rubber bands. My eyes bulged wide open. His confidence and demeanor impressed me, so I had nothing to say.

"Buckle your seat belt, baby. I'm bout to spend all this money on my new girl."

I couldn't do anything but smile and buckle up. If I knew then what I know now, I would have been running for the hills.

When we got to Concord Mall, it wasn't too crowded. We went in H&M and Jazzy bought six outfits for me. I got some nice shirts with skinny jeans and purses to match. I just knew we were meant to be together. I had a great feeling about him.

"Let's go into Victoria's Secret."

"Really, Jazzy?"

"Yeah, I got to hook my shawty up right. You know I'm going marry you one day, right?"

Given the fact that we'd just met, I shot him a crazy look and laughed in his face.

"I'm serious, but I know that things don't happen overnight."

"Either you're crazy or you're really feeling me."

"Karmen, I'll go with the second one."

He leaned in for a kiss on my smooth lips and my panties started to drip a little. I mean, Jazon was too fine to not see if what he says would manifest. Who knows, he could be my husband. We walked into the store all of the sweet scents and perfumes that filled the air amazed me.

"Karmen put everything that you want in this bag and I got you, boo." Pear Glace and Love Spell instantly came to mind. I put six bottles of each in the bag and Jazzy smiled at me.

"What?"

"Nothing, boo...go over there and try on some lingerie, too."

"Are you serious?" I couldn't help but grin after I said it. I felt like a kid in a candy store, just picking up everything and being able to get it. I looked at the lingerie and tried on a red-laced halter-top nightie with matching thongs.

"Damn, Karmen...you will look good in that?"

"You think so?" I said as I winked at him.

"Go try it on and let's see."

I walked up to the sales clerk who had been looking at us since we showed up in the store and asked her for a key.

"Miss, I would like to try this on in the dressing room, please."

"Uh, sure ma'am, no problem." Her accent was British and she had black hair with freckles on her face. I went into the dressing room and tried on the lingerie.

"Well, what do you think?"

I was sashaying around in the dressing room like I was Tyra Banks walking on the catwalk during Fashion Week.

"Damn, shawty...you got a sexy body!" Jazzy started licking his lips and rubbing his hands together at the same time.

"I take it that you like?"

"Yea, we are definitely going to cop that."

"Okay, then."

After I said that, he leaned in and kissed me. I kissed him back and instantly got moist. I pushed him out of the dressing room so that I could go change.

"Go," I said, laughing. "I have to get changed so we could go."

"Okay, okay," he said playfully. He paid for my things and then we got back in the car and went back in town.

"So, you gon' be my main girl, right?"

I raised a brow as we were on 202 at the light.

"How about your only girl? If not, then we can just part ways and I can do me."

"Yeah, okay. I'll snap if I see my girl with another dude on her arm."

I smiled and blushed at the same time. I had never gotten in a relationship so quickly before. I mean, usually we were friends first; then dating and then the relationship. I should have questioned the sudden rush, but it felt right, so I went with it.

"Okay, baby. I have to take care of some business, so where do you live?"

"I live on 5th and Monroe."

"Really?"

"Yes, really...why you say it like that?" I started to quickly get offended, being as though he met me not even a block away from where I live.

"Naw, it ain't like that, lil' mama...calm down." He saw the expression on my face. "It's just that is where my coworkers be, so now I'll make sure that they look out for you."

"Look out for me?"

"Yes. You my girl now, so I gotta keep you safe." Jazzy realized that he slipped up when he said that because my voice started to rise and I was getting pissed off.

"Look, Jazzy. I don't know what you and your drug dealers are into, but I want no parts. So, with that being said..."

Before I could say another word, he had pulled over by on the curb across the street from the liquor store on 4th street.

"Karmen, it's not like that, baby. It's just that I want you to be safe now that you my boo. I don't sell drugs, but I do have people that sell them for me. I just don't want anything to happen to you."

"Why would something happing to me?" I started to cry thinking that someone could actually want to hurt me.

"Baby, stop crying. No one is going to hurt you. I will make sure of that. It's just that people will know you're my girl and may try and get with you, and I will have to fuck them up."

We both laughed as Jazzy wiped my tears with his thumb. He started the car back up and kept driving until we got to my house.

"This is you, aye?"

"Yup, this is me."

"You stay here by yourself?"

"Yes, I do."

"Okay, cool...go head in the house and I'll call you later."

"Yes, sir." I said while saluting his dominance.

We shared a kissed as I got all of my bags and went in the house. Jazzy waited until I closed the door to pull off. I dropped my bags on my couch and headed upstairs to take a nap. Putting my cell phone on the charger, I turned on my radio and listened to "Lost without You" by Robin Thick as I took my clothes off and drifted into a deep sleep.

When I woke up about two hours later, I checked my cell phone and noticed that I had two missed calls from Jazzy. I walked downstairs to grab a bowl of cereal and I heard a knock on my door.

"Who is it?"

"Meana."

I opened the door and my best friend entered my house. We both screamed because we hadn't seen each other since graduation, which was about six months ago.

"Meanaaaaaaaaaaaaaaaaaaaaaa."

"Hey, Karmen!""Girl there is never any parking around here." Meana said.

"Tell me about it."

"So, what's new?" Karmen

"Well, I still haven't found a job, but I did meet someone!" Giggling like two schoolgirls, we both curled up on my couch like old times. I had forgotten to bring my bags upstairs and put the clothes and other things away.

"Karmen, where did you get all this stuff from?"

"My new boo, Jazon, aka Jazzy, bought it."

"Jazzy? What kind of name is that? Okay, Karmen, tell me how you met him. Spill your guts."

"Okay, okay," I said, laughing uncontrollably. "Earlier today, I was walking down the street and stopped for a second to send a text to my dad. Anyway, I noticed this guy staring at me, and he looked good. "

"Damn, he must have been feeling you to have gotten you all this stuff."

"Meana, I'm fly as shit...why wouldn't he like me." We both started laughing again. "Okay let me finish telling you the story before I forget."

"Okay, go 'head, Karmen." She leaned in, ready for me to finish the conversation.

"So, we were talking and he asked me where I was headed. I told him the mall. He offered to take me as he pulled out all this money."

"Say word, Karmen?"

"Yes, girl...no bullshit!"

"Wow, you lucked up."

"Who you telling, Meana?"

"I think that this will be a good thing , Meana."

Meana and I sat for about two hours and talked about our college days. She told me that she was in love with her boyfriend. I was happy to be chilling with one of my good friends. In the back of my mind, I still wondered why Jazzy called me twice and didn't leave a message. As I listened to Meana go on and on about her boo, I got a text message from Jazzy.

"Hey Gorgeous."

"Hey Jazzy, what's up?"

"You are, shawty."

"Oh really?"

"Yeah...want to go to dinner tonight?"

"Yes, what time?"

"Be ready at 7pm."

"Okay."

When I looked at my phone, time had gone by so quickly; it was already six o'clock.

"Meana, girl, we have got to take a rain check because I have a date."

"With who...Jazzy?"

We both started laughing as she put on her shoes, getting ready to leave. We gave our hugs and said our goodbyes and she left. I ran upstairs to look in my closet. I didn't know what to wear for the date

"What do I wear?" I scanned my closet so fast that I grabbed the first not-so-revealing dress that I could find; a red spaghetti-strapped dress that would hug my scrumptious curves just in the right places and have my cleavage showing just a little. I held the dress, still on its hanger, in my hands.

"Jazzy, I gotta leave something for the imagination, now. Can't have you looking at all my goodies on the first date."

I don't know who I was kidding; the chemistry was so strong that he could get it tonight if he really wanted it. Running my bubble bath, I got undressed. Rubbing Noxzema all over my face, I quickly got in the tub. The water was still a little hot, so I had to grab onto the sides of the tub and slowly squatted.

"Oh, shit, hot...hot!" I said it like I had just walked over hot coals. That's what it felt like as I eased down in the tub. I laid my head back and relaxed while I thought about Jazzy.

Is he the one for me? Why do I feel so strongly about him and I hardly know him? There were so many thoughts going through my head because I had never felt this way about any guy this quickly. I quickly washed my body with my loofah and washed the Noxzema off my face. With my yellow towel wrapped around me, I fixed my hair. I had put in pin curls yesterday, and it still looked great. I usually never pinned my hair up. It looked like I never had it done around the second day or so. I quickly put my dress on and looked in the mirror just one more time before I headed downstairs. My favorite shoes were in the closet. They were red open-toe heels that were about three inches high. I loved to wear heels. They always gave me the perfect posture when walking. Sitting down stairs, I suddenly heard a knock on my door.

"Oh my God, he's here."

Before I opened the door, my stomach was filled with butterflies. I was so excited and anxious to be going on a date because it had been so long. When I opened the door, Jazzy was wearing a nice black sweater with blue jeans and a black pair of Stacy Adams. He pulled the outfit off perfectly.

"Hey, sexy."

"Hey, Jazzy."

"These are for you."

"Awww Thank, you sweetie."

Jazzy had gotten me some beautiful long stemmed red roses. I couldn't believe it because they were so nice. I hurried to the kitchen to put the flowers in some water, and from the corner of my eye, I noticed Jazzy checking out my house.

"Baby, you have a gorgeous house, here."

"Thanks."

"I love the artwork that you have on your wall, and your brown sectional gives it a nice touch."

"Why, thank you. Are you ready to go?"

"Yup."

Heading out the door, I made sure that my door was closed tight as I locked it. Looking around at my neighbors, I saw them look at us as we got in the car. I hated the fact that they were so nosey.

"Your neighbors know you messin' with a boss, shawty!"

"Yeah, I see."

"By the way, you look real sexy in that dress. Am I going to get a chance to take it off with my teeth?"

I couldn't help but blush and smile when he said that, but I had to be a lady. I was not giving it up, even though I wanted to so bad. I mean, hell, he was fine and hell, and not to mention, he seemed to be crazy about me.

"I don't think so."

"It was worth a try." He winked at me and smiled.

"Where are we going, anyway?"

"We are headed to an Italian restaurant in Jersey called Enzo's...ever been?"

"No, but I heard that it was a great place to eat."

"We gon' find out, boo."

I sat in the car just day-dreaming about how I had found the perfect man. I never thought that I would meet anyone like him. As I was looking out the window, we had hopped on 202, passing the Concord Mall and Target. I must have been too quiet because I didn't even hear Jazzy call my name.

"Karmen...helloooo, Karmen."

"Oh, I'm sorry, sweetie...what's up?"

"You alright, shawty?"

"Yes, I'm fine. I was just thinking."

"'Bout what?"

I had to think of something and quick. I couldn't let him know that I was thinking about him and a possible future that I wanted us to have.

"I was just thinking about how I'm looking for a job now that I have finished school."

"Well, I think of it like this; now that you are with me, you don't have to work."

Both of my eyebrows rose.

"Come again?"

"Look, Karmen. You my girl and don't have to work. I got you on the bills, hair, nails, tuition, and everything."

"Jazzy, that's nice and all, but I didn't go to school to not have to work."

"I understand that, boo, but I don't want my girl worrying over getting a job when you don't have to."

"Well I'm thinking about going back to school to get my Master's degree in Psychology."

"Okay, you do that. I will pay for everything, books, and the whole nine."

"Really?"

"Yes, Karmen, why is it so hard for you to believe that your mine? We are going to be together for ever...watch."

"Okay, Jazzy."

"Just let me know how much your bills average out to a month and how much the tuition is for the year and I'll pay it."

"Okay."

I couldn't wait until I got home to call Meana and tell her this shit. I had truly hit the jackpot with this man. My plan was to ride this until the wheels fall off.

"Karmen reach in the back seat, and get the red duffle bag and open it up. I want you to have what's in there."

"Uh...okay." I was a little hesitant.

I hurried up and got the bag because I wanted to know what was in the bag. It seems that Jazzy was quite the surprising type. I had to admit that I loved every minute of it. With the duffle bag on my lap, I opened it up and there was money everywhere. My eyes grew big like diamonds sparkling because I just couldn't believe all the money that was wrapped in rubber bands.

"Karmen, I want you to have all that."

"Oh my God, how much is in here?"

"It's only 5,000 dollars."

"Only?!"

"That's half of what I made last year when I was working." Chuckling, Jazzy then pulled up into Enzo's. With my mind still in shock, I stayed frozen in the car.

"Jazzy, did you rob a bank or something?"

"No." He started laughing.

"I don't want drug money, either." I said.

By this time, my mouth frowned and my arms were folded. I couldn't believe that he had expected me to take all of this money. *I mean, he could at least give me a check*, I thought to myself.

"Karmen it's not drug money. I got this from my checking account."

"Whatever, Jazzy. Let's just go in and eat."

"No, we're not going anywhere until you hear me out." He raised his voice a little bit.

"I'm listening, Jazzy."

"Good. Let me make myself clear. This money is not drug money, and I'm giving it to you because I want you to be straight. Any girl would love to be in your shoes right now." He had a good point. A lot of girls would love to be in my position.

"Baby, come here." Jazzy leaned in and gave me a kiss and I felt a lot better. We stayed lip-locked for a while and finally went in to the restaurant. When we walked into the restaurant, I couldn't believe my eyes. The restaurant had a lovely romantic setting. There were small round tables with red tablecloths and with a tea candle in the center of each table. There were booths, available as well. I couldn't believe how intimate the setting was.

"It's just the two of you?" the waiter asked as we walked up to the podium where he met us.

"Yes, just us two. And if you don't mind, could we have a booth?"

"Yes, ma'am."

I wanted us to be as private as possible so I could talk with Jazzy and get to know him more without a lot of interruptions. We were seated at the booth and the waiter handed us menus.

"So Jazzy, tell me more about you."
Taking his coat off, he looked at me with a
puzzled look.

"Well, let's see. I'm from Atlanta and
I am an only child."

"Wow, were you spoiled as a kid?"

"Not really. I started making my own
money when I was young."

"Let me guess...you had people
working for you then."

"Yes, men and women."

"Women? What did they do?"

"They make money for me...that's all you need to know."

"Okay then."

After he said that, I began to wonder. *What in hell did the women do to make him money?* Looking over the menu, Jazzy spoke again.

"So, Karmen what are you getting?"

"I think I'm going to have the chicken Parmesan with spaghetti...what about you?"

"I'm going to have some shrimp Alfredo."

"Mmm, that sounds good."

The waiter came back over to take our orders.

"Have you two decided on what you will have for dinner and drinks?"

"Yes. Karmen, you go first."

"Oh okay. I'll have the chicken Parmesan with spaghetti and a sweet tea."

"Very good choice, ma'am. And you, sir?"

"I'll get the shrimp Alfredo with a sweet tea, also."

"Very good. I will be back with your orders shortly."

Once the waiter walked away, I wanted to talk to Jazzy about the money that he gave me. I still was surprised that he gave me 5,000 dollars.

"Babe, what am I suppose to do with all that money?"

"Spend it, Karmen. Buy you a car, or pay bills...whatever you want, babe."

I sighed deeply and could tell that Jazzy was annoyed by my reactions to the money.

"Look, Karmen. You have to stop worrying about the money and just enjoy it, okay, baby?"

"Okay."

He leaned over the table and gave me a kiss. I must admit that I was so turned on by the way his lips felt against mines. Moments later, our food and drinks were served. I was hungry, so I started eating very quickly.

"Damn, shawty, slow down. I ain't going to eat your food," he said, laughing.

"Oh, I know. I'm hungry. I hadn't eaten all day for some reason."

"It's all good baby girl; eat until your heart is content." We both laughed while we ate. Moments later, we were both full and ready to go.

"Baby girl, you ready to go?"

"Yes, I'm so full, it doesn't make any sense."

"Okay." Jazzy paid the bill and we headed to the car back to Delaware.

"Did you enjoy yourself, baby?"

"I did," I said as I held his hand while he drove. It felt so natural being with him that I was starting to get scared. This was all happening to quickly. I mean, I had just met him, and yet, we were inseparable. Pulling up in front of my house, there was no parking spot once again. We ended up parking all the way on the corner and had to walk up the hill, which I hated. Walking to my steps, my heart started racing a mile a minute.

"Am I allowed to come in?" This scenario felt like I was Nina in the movie, *Love Jones*, when Darius was on Nina's steps wanting to come into her house.

"Oh I don't know...my man might get mad," I said as I winked at him.

"Fuck yo' man. I'll take you from him." After he said that, he couldn't help but laugh as I unlocked the door. Once inside, Jazzy helped me out of my coat.

"Damn, Karmen...you really look good in that dress, babe."

"Thank you."

"It's a shame that I won't see you in it for too long."

I started feeling on his muscular chest through the black sweater that he was wearing as we engaged in a passionate kiss. Jazzy quickly lifted me up and carried me upstairs.

"Which way to the bedroom, baby?"

"The door on the left." When we reached our destination, Jazzy's mouth dropped from the look of my room. I had white carpet all over with a king-size bed with the poles going up on each side. My bed was in the center, while on the left had side, I had a rocking chair with a pink teddy bear sitting in it. On the right side were my dresser and a small end table with fake roses in the vase. . Right above my bed, I had a big, nude self-portrait that my friend had drawn of me when he was taking art in college. The red curtains accented my room beautifully. Cinnamon filled the air, due to the Glade Plug-Ins that I had all over the entire room.

"Wow, baby...now this is a woman's room!"

"Good. Now, are you going to place me on the bed any time soon?" Still having me in his arms, I was started to get a little stiff just being in one spot. He carefully placed me on the bed and I turned on my Pandora. The song, "Can I Come Over" by Aaliyah, started playing, so I knew the mood was set right. I jumped off the bed and went into the bathroom where I left the lingerie and the pumps that we had gotten earlier.

"Stay right here. I will be right back."

"Okay, boo."

Jazzy was still looking around my room in adoration as he began to undress. I washed my under arms and my kitty hurriedly so that I would be fresh for Jazzy. Now, I know that I should have at least given it a month, but this just felt right. I know that it has only been a day, but my heart felt right about this guy...or did it? I mean, he bought me clothes and gave me thousands of dollars all in one day. What was he up to? He just really likes me and wants me for me. I got my negative thoughts out of the way and focused on the positive. Looking at myself in the mirror, I looked sexy as shit.

Okay, Karmen. Go show your man how much you really appreciate all that he does for you, I thought to myself. I walked into the doorway with my legs spread and strutted into the room.

"Damn, shawty!"

All of a sudden, R. Kelly's "Seem Like You're Ready" started to play. Once I heard that, it was my cue to give Jazzy a show that he would never forget. Gliding my body and swerving my hips to the music, Jazzy was in pure de lust. Dancing slowly to the music, I dropped down to the floor, did a split, and bought my body back up and climbed on one of the poles on my bed. Grabbing my hair with both of my hands and rotating my butt in a sexy demeanor, Jazzy's friend was standing at attention. The music was still playing, and by this time, I had started to take the thong off, throwing it at Jazzy. Next, I took off the corset top and tossed it on the floor. By this time, Jazzy couldn't take it and was pinning for me as he grabbed me. Falling on top of him, I couldn't help but smile seductively. He turned me over and started to suck on my nipples slowly as they became erect from his tender touch.

"Damn Karmen, you are so sexy."

"Am I?" I asked in between breaths from the pleasure I was receiving with his wet, juicy tongue. Scrolling down like he was a mouse on a computer, he moved to my navel and started kissing it and licking slowly. My center was leaking at this point. I moved my hand down there to pleasure myself.

"Oh, don't worry...that pretty pussy is going to be fed. Believe that," he said.

He then teased my pearl with his index finger before placing his body down to my cat, front and center. Tasting what my center had to offer, my body tensed up as I grabbed on his head with my left hand

and clinched the sheet with the other. I was in pure bliss.

"Jazzy that feels so good, baby."

"Its tastes as good as it feels," he said in between eating dinner..

My breathing was uncontrollable, and before I knew it, I was climaxing all in Jazzy's mouth. Someone would have thought that he was drinking the milk from a bowl of cereal because he didn't budge from having me. Coming up for air, he spoke.

"Damn, that was better than the shrimp Alfredo."

In such a daze, I couldn't say anything. I could only continue breathing through the great orgasm that I had.

"Okay, let me taste your lollipop so you can tell me how many licks it takes to get to the center."

"Damn, right. I love that shit."

As Jazzy lay on the bed, I kissed him from head to navel, as he did me. I then slowly placed my lips on his hard stiff vessel. Moaning in ecstasy, I felt his legs trembling. When I looked up at him, his eyes were rolling in the back of his head while he was shaking uncontrollably. I deep throated him and created the humming effect and that drove him up the wall.

"Damn, Karmen...oh my god."

He quickly grabbed me and put me on the bed. Before I knew it, he entered me and I felt all of his hardness slip inside of me because I was so wet.

"Ahhh, Jazzy...that feels so good."

"Damn right, it does."

"My clients are going to love this pussy."

"Clients?"

I was no longer in the mood once he said that because I had no idea what he was talking about.

"Jazzy, what do you mean by 'clients'?"

Ignoring me, Jazzy kept on pumping me harder. I lost my train of thought as I moaned even louder.

"Ahhh."

"Damn, this pussy is so right."

All of a sudden, Jazzy yelled, "You're my main girl, right?"

"Mmmm, yes daddy...the main and only girl."

While he was fucking me out of control, I came all over his dick.

"That's right, baby...cum all on this dick."

"Jaaazzzzyyyy, mmmm...I'm cuuummmming!"

I had my last orgasm of the night. Breathing heavily, I turned to my side and lay on the bed. Jazzy lay next to me.

"You know you got a secret weapon there, right?"

"That's what they say."

"They?"

"Boy, don't trip. You don't think my pussy is this good being a virgin, do you?"

"Oh, I feel you."

"Well, I'm glad that you liked it."

"Me too."

"Come here." Jazzy said.

I slid my body over by Jazzy and lay on his chest. It was the most peaceful thing in the world to just lie on a man's chest. We were up for hours, just laying in bed and talking about our childhoods, when Jazzy's phone rang. He looked at the number and picked it up right away.

"Yo, what's good, ma?"

I sat up in bed while he was sitting up sideways taking his call.

"What you mean he didn't want to pay all of the money upfront?"

I was wondering who didn't want to pay their money and why Jazzy had women selling drugs.

"Yo, shawty, for real. I'm not playing. You better get my fucking money." He seemed to get real upset at this girl for some reason. "Look here. Be clear, shut up, and listen to me."

I could hear the girl in the background saying obliging.

"If you don't have my money by the time I'm ready to collect, there are going to be some issues."

What kind of issues, I thought.

I was beginning to get worried, so I tapped Jazzy on the shoulder, but he waved his finger in the air, signaling me to wait until he was done with his call.

"Okay, shawty, that's cool. We have no problems and working double is cool with me. Well I'm here with my girl right now, so I'll holla back at you." I could hear the girl on the other end of the phone.

"Your girl?"

She sounded angry, and before she could say anything else, Jazzy hung up the phone.

"Jazzy, I don't get into your business, but what was that about?"

"Ugh...one of my coworkers was robbed and they took her product, so she's working over time to get my money."

"What issues was she going to have if she didn't have your money?"

"She isn't going to have any issues. I don't hit women or anything. I just said that to scare her."

"Well, it worked on me, and I'm not even an employee. That phone call was crazy, for real."

"Baby, it's cool; she's just going to work overtime. Besides, she's being paid, too."

"Okay, well, maybe you should not scare your employees."

"Baby, I won't do that anymore. I promise."

"Good...now go to sleep."

Jazzy fell asleep within minutes, but I was still up. The phone call that I heard made me think that Jazzy was hiding something. I was going to get to the bottom of it. Meanwhile, I had some new things to buy with the money that I had just acquired. As far as Jazzy was concerned, I would soon find out what was up with him. My momma always said, "What's done in the dark will come to light." Eventually, time would tell the story.

Part 2

After The Fact

It was a week later and I was still wondering about that phone call Jazzy received at my house. We had just had a great night, and suddenly, a woman called his phone talking about money that she was supposed to make for him. I know that he told me that he sold drugs, but there was more to the story.

I ended up buying a car with the money that Jazzy gave me. That's right, a two-door, blue Honda accord. I was at the red light on DuPont Highway going to register for school

when Jazzy called me. The ringtone, "My Boo"
by Alicia Keys and Usher, was playing.

*"I remember when we were younger, you
were my...my boo!"*

"Hello?"

"Karmen, where you at, babe?"

"On my way to school to sign up for classes.
What are you up to?"

"I'm at work. Do you want to watch a movie
later at my house?"

"Sure, baby, that sounds like
fun...what time?" It was a little
suspicious that he   didn't come
over my house like usual, but I was cool
with it.

"Let's make it 10pm."

"Okay. I'll see you later tonight."

We both hung up the phone. I had never been over Jazzy's house, so I couldn't wait to see what it looked like. Things between us were great. I got money a lot from Jazzy and we always went out and spent time together. We clicked so well that it felt like we had been together longer. I finally arrived at school and prepared for the long registration process.

"Welcome to the graduate center. How can I help you?"

"Yes, my name is Karmen Watson and I'm here for a meeting with an advisor."

"Okay, Ms. Watson, can I get your student I.D number?"

"29735," I said asI stood at the front desk while he looked up my information.

"Okay, Ms. Watson, have a seat and your advisor will come and get you."

"Thank you." I sat down and looked my phone because it just vibrated. I had gotten a text from Jazzy.

"Hey, on your way to my crib, bring some lingerie because I want to do the photo shoot that I was telling you about. Don't worry. I'm the one that will be taking the pictures."

"Jazzy, that sounds fun and sexy. Will do...see you later. Love you."

"Love you, too."

I met with my advisor and signed up for four classes, which totaled four thousand dollars. I was happy that I was able to pay my tuition with my debit card. I didn't want to wait in the long line for my books, so I opted to just buy them online and have them shipped to my house and left the school.

When I got home, I noticed that there was a woman standing in front on my house. She was dressed provocatively with her short black skirt and you can see her ass. Not to mention the red belly shirt and her stomach had the most hideous stretch marks, with bright red lipstick. She was a chocolate girl with a short, Toni Braxton-like haircut . I was a little nervous not knowing why she was standing in front of my house.

"Excuse me...are you Karmen?"

"Who wants to know?" I looked her up and down, prepared for anything that she tried. I rolled my eyes and mean-mugging her, thinking, *Bitch, I wish you would try something.*

"Relax, sweetie. I just wanted to ask you about Jazzy. I know that you're his main girl now, and I wanted you to tell him that I quit."

"Quit what? And how did you know where I lived?"

"Everyone knows where you live." I quickly raised a brow because I was so confused. "Karmen, the whole block and then some knows about you and Jazzy."

"Oh okay. I'm sorry, but why are you here?"

"I told you that I wanted you to tell him that I, Jenny, quit."

"Shouldn't you be telling him that? I don't get involved in his business."

"Oh, so you mean to tell me that you aren't working for him and giving him the money you make?"

My eyes grew wide because this Jenny girl had clearly stepped out of bounds. I was about to give her a piece of my mind when Jazzy's car pulled up in front of my house. He got out the car so fast that I didn't know what was going to happen.

"What's up, boo?" he said to me with a concerned look on his face.

"You tell me...why is this Jenny girl coming at my crib telling me to tell you that she quits?" Once I said that, Jenny had a look of fear in her eyes.

"Alright, Karmen, go in the house. I'll take care of it."

"No, Jazzy, I need an explanation as to why she came to my house." All of a sudden, Jazzy yelled at me in front of all the neighbors who were around.

"Karmen, I said get in the damn house! I'll handle it!"

I got my purse and went in the house like I was told. I tried to look out of my window so that I could hear what he would say to her, but he grabbed her and they walked down the street. I went back outside and heard everything.

"Yo, Jenny, what's good with you showing up at my girl's crib?" He grabbed Jenny by the arm and squeezed it tight. Jenny started to cry.

"I just had to see who you left me for."

"Left you for? Bitch, I was never with you."

"What, Jazzy? You going to say that after all we have been through? All the money that I made and the people that you made me sleep with?"

"Yo, bitch, you work for me, and you will continue to work for me until you are finished making my money."

Jazzy looked like he was about to hit her, but instead, he pulled her close and hugged her. Jenny wiped her tears and started to walk away when I ran back in the house and turned the TV on. Jazzy soon followed.

"Karmen, I need to talk to you about that."

I folded my arms with my eyes glued to him.

"Uh, yes you do, 'cause that was some bullshit, for real!"

"Bottom line, she is a coworker and we used to date. She's still in love with me."

"Jazzy, I don't care that y'all dated, but why did she come to my house?"

"Everyone knows you're my girl, so she just showed up. Trust me, it won't happen again." I wasn't buying his story at all.

"Are you ready to go to my house?"

"No, I'm not."

He sat next to me on the couch and kissed me. I couldn't help but to kiss him back. In that moment, I was no longer mad at Jazzy. He started to put his hand under my shirt and through my bra, touching my nipples.

"Mmm...Jazzy, stop." I had started to laugh, but I was loving it.

"You know you don't want me to stop, Karmen." Jazzy said in a seductive tone.

Without hesitation, Jazzy pulled down my jeans and panties and entered my center with his tongue for a little snack. As he licked my insides, I couldn't help but to shake.

"Ohhhh, Jazzy, that feels soo good!"

As he continued to eat, I could feel two fingers being placed inside me. Getting wetter and wetter, I thought that I was going to explode on his face.

"Aaahhhhh...aaahhh...I think I'm about to cum."

As soon as those words parted my lips, Jazzy pulled his pants down and entered me. Pumping and thrusting inside of me, my kitten had left like it was taking a terrible beating..

"Damn, this pussy is so fucking wet." Jazzy said.

"Uughh...uughh...Jazzy, I love you," I said in between moans. I couldn't help that I was so in love with this man. It was like he had me hypnotized.

"I love you too, Karmen."

Before I knew it, I was being turned over on the couch with my knees resting on the couch and my face down in the pillow.

"That's right...you know how I like it...face down and ass up."

I started to get a little annoyed because, while he was entering me from behind, I could feel his sweat drip on my back and that made me feel so nasty. As he smacked me on my big ass, the sweat just kept dripping on me like it was drizzling rain outside.

Oh my god, this is so nasty, I thought to myself.

With my mind deflected off the sex and on to Jazzy's sweat, I started to get out of the mood and my kitty started dry up like the Sahara desert. Jazzy noticed the quick change.

"Karmen, don't get dry on me now. Throw that ass back on this dick just like you like it."

"Okay."

"Okay, what?"

"Okay, daddy."

Ever since the first time that we had sex, he told to call him 'daddy'. I though that it was stupid, but, hey, some men liked that, I guess.

"Mmmm, daddy it feels so good."

"Come on, Karmen talk to me...what feels good?"

Trying to catch my breath, I was now back in the mood. I hated when we would ask questions during sex. I mean, sometimes, it was sexy, but right about now, it was all about getting a nut.

"Daddy, your dick feels so good inside me."

I started to throw my ass back on his dick, just the way that he liked it. When I increased my speed and developed my own rhythm, he started to moan loudly.

"Daddy, it feels good to you?"

"Hell yeah, it does!"

"You gon' cum for me, daddy?" He started smacking my ass again, and this time, for some reason, I loved every minute of it.

"Daddy, I'm cummminng! I'm cummming!"

"Cum all on this big dick. Ohhh shit, Karmen. Damn, baby!"

We climaxed at the same time. I couldn't believe that we didn't even get the chance to make it upstairs.

"That was fun, Jazzy."

"I'm glad you enjoyed it."

"Let's go get a shower and get ready for the photo shoot that I want to do."

"Why are you so hyped about this photo shoot?" I asked as we both headed upstairs to get in the shower.

"I can't take sexy pictures of my baby?"
"Jazzy, I ain't say that, but you're just so persistent about this."

"I want you to dance for me, too."

"Okay, I guess."

I was thinking to myself, *what was he up to, wanting me to dance and do a photo shoot for him? I mean, I love to experience new things, but something doesn't sit right with me.*

Once we showered, I packed an overnight bag and some lingerie for the *photo shoot.*

"Karmen, I'm going to the car. Hurry up. I got your bags, boo."

Okay, Jazzy, I'm coming. I'm just making sure I got everything."

"You don't because I have everything."

I locked up the house and we headed to Jazzy's house.

Lights, Camera, Action

When we got to Jazzy's house, I thought I was in a photographer's studio. He had it all decked out. He had a bed, couch, the camera with the stand, and different backgrounds with the lights to match the perfect setting. He had a big loft decorated nicely. It wasn't bad for a man's pad.

"You like it, shawty?"

"Like? Try love! I didn't know that you were in photography."

"Yeah, it's a lot you don't know about me, but you will soon find out."

I didn't know if that was a good or bad thing. I mean, I liked learning about him and seeing what other talents that he had.

"Alright, sweetie, go in the bathroom and get changed so we can knock this shoot out right quick and then curl up in bed and watch a movie."

"Mmm, sounds good to me."

I walked in his bathroom and his tub was gorgeous! It looked like the kind of bathtub that was used during the ancient times; so big and round. I was guaranteed to bathe in it. I slipped into my baby blue bra and boy shorts set with a small robe to match.

"How do I look?"

"Damn, you got my dick hard. Okay, now position yourself on the bed and we can get started."

"Okay."

I got on the bed and began provocatively posing for Jazzy. First, I stood up on my knees with both hands on my head and he snapped the picture.

"That's hot, babe!" Jazzy shouted as he snapped away.

Then, I lay on the bed with one leg perched winking and smiling at him.

"Okay, Karmen, now stand by the background and let's do a couple poses there."

I did as I was told, wondering what he was going to do with the pictures. I mean, all this to keep to himself?

Two outfits later, I was still taking pictures. It started to get annoying for me because I was getting a little tired.

"Babe, are we done? I'm getting tired."

"Yes, sweetie...we are finished."

"Finally! What are you going to do with the pictures, anyway?"

"Well, I'm going to make you a model."

I started getting excited again because, since I was a child, I always wanted to model.

"Okay, what kind of modeling?"

"Well, I may have you dance for clients so that they can get a look at your figure."

"I'm not going to be a stripper, Jazzy."

"Okay, but you can dance, babe. You could make a lot of money dancing and modeling. You'd be killing two birds with one stone."

We sat on the couch and turned Netflix on. The idea that Jazzy had for me did cross my mind. I could dance and model part-time while going to school full-time. Laying on Jazzy, we chose to watch my all-time favorite movie, "The Lost Boys".

"Jazzy, I will think about it. I want to see the pictures first."

"Okay, babe. Let's watch the movie."

Two hours later, the movie had ended and we had both fallen asleep in each other's arms. I woke up to turned off the TV and then got in his bed. When I woke up about an hour later, the smell of food filled the air. The smell of bacon, pancakes, and eggs hit my nostrils.

"Hey babe…good morning." Jazzy was so happy and chipper. "I made you breakfast."

"Oh really?" I started to chuckle. He gave me a kiss on the cheek.

"Yes, and while you eat, you can look at the pictures that I developed."

I sat at his nice dining table. I felt that I was Vivian Ward on the movie, "Pretty Woman", because Jazzy's spread was almost as big as Edward's. There were pancakes, bacon, eggs, muffins, and fresh fruit. I cut my pancakes up into squares while I slowly poured some Aunt Jemima syrup on them. My pictures were in a nice little portfolio packet.

"Wow, babe...these are really nice!"

"I told you that you are beautiful and you take great pictures, Karmen."

"Thanks, Babe."

The rest of the morning went well with Jazzy and me. We went shopping for some outfits for me to dance and model in. I was, indeed, a little nervous, but I was ready to go. This was my time to shine, so let the games begin.

"It's My Time To Shine"

The moment had finally come and it was my night to dance at Club X. I was dressed in my sexy nurse outfit with the matching bra and panty set underneath. I was nervous but ready to go. There were so many other girls that were in the dressing room, all of them staring at me up and down. I guess I looked better than them. Rubbing my shoulders, Jazzy I could hear Jazzy speak.

"Baby, are you ready?"

"No, I'm a nervous wreck and my palms are sweating."

"You will be fine. Wait until after your performance, I got a surprise for you, but what I want you to trust me okay?"

"Okay."

Girls were coming exiting the stage left and right. As I paid closer attention to them, I noticed that they were holding their clothes in their hand. I thought, *what the fuck? I thought that the dancers were just dancing and getting off the stage. I didn't think that they were stripping.*

"Jazzy, we have an issue," I said. He was talking to a man when I rudely interrupted him.

"What's wrong babe?"

"What's wrong is you didn't tell me that I would taking my clothes off. I thought that I was just dancing and the men would be taking the pictures...that's all."

"Karmen are you serious?" Jazzy said sarcastically, laughing.

"Does it look like I'm laughing, Jazzy?"

"What did you think dancing was? Of course you are going to take your clothes off, baby. A lot of my clients want to see what you are working with."

I started to cry as he spoke. I felt blindsided and I started to not recognize this man who was so nice and good to me almost a month ago.

"Jazzy, I'm not doing this." I stood up and was ready to walk out when Jazzy forcefully grabbed, me hurting my arm.

"Jazzy, you are hurting me."

"Look here, Karmen. I have a lot of money riding on this performance, so you will take your fucking clothes off, or else!"

I began to cry even harder. Jazzy grabbed the back of my neck so tight that I knew I would have a bruise in the morning.

"Look at how pretty you look, baby. You don't want to mess up your makeup with all those tears, do you?"

"No," I said in between sobs.

"Good. Now get up there and make daddy proud."

Getting myself together, I reapplied the red lipstick that I had chosen to wear. This dance would no longer be fun for me anymore. I watched as another dancer exited the stage. I was up next. I listened to the announcer as he introduced me.

"Gentlemen we have a new fish here in Club X, and she's a nurse. Not just any nurse, but Nurse Karmen!! If you need your temperature taken, she is the nurse for the job." I could hear the men scream as I went on stage. The song I chose was "T-shirt and My Panties" by Adina Howard.

"Yeahhhh...oh, she's sexy!" I heard a man say. He put a $20 bill up on the stage just as I started to sashay around the pole. I had taken some pole dancing lessons with Meana for fun, so I'm glad that I had that to fall back on. While I was dancing, I had so much on my mind with Jazzy and school. During the middle of the song, I climbed up the stripper pole and slid back down slowly. The crowd was going crazy. Swaying my hips from side to side I started to take the nurse uniform started to come off.

"Damn, I want to fuck her," I heard a man yell from the crowd while he was making it rain right in front of me. I walked up to him with a sexy attitude and started picking up the money while winking at him. In reality, I wanted to puke and spit in his face. I felt degraded and wished I had the guts to just leave the club. The song was finally over and I had made $400 for just that night.

"Damn, boo, you did good!"

"Thanks Jazzy...can we go now?"

"Can we go? No baby, we still have more money to make."

"How, Jazzy? I did my dance for the night and I'm tired."

"Come on. I just need you to do one more thing. You do love me, don't you?"

He had started flashing that sexy smile that drove me crazy. The way his lips curled when he'd kiss me was one of the things that made me fall for him.

"Okay, what do I have to do?"

"Make a thousand dollars because one of my other employees had to cancel."

"Well, what do I have to do?"

"Sleep with him and bring me money."

I couldn't believe he just said that like it was nothing. How disrespectful was that of him to think that he could just ask me to sleep with another man?

"Sleep with him?"

"Come on, Karmen. You're a smart girl."

"If I'm a smart girl, why would you want me to make a dumb decision?" Before I knew it, Jazzy smacked me in the face so hard that it started to throb. I never thought that he would ever hit me.

"What the fuck?" I said.

Suddenly, he hit me again. I couldn't believe it. Jazzy never came off as the type to abuse women; it just didn't seem to fit in his character.

"Why would you hit me?" I tearfully asked him.

"Baby, I'm sorry, but you have to listen to me. I know what's best for you." I just sat in the chair and held my face with my hand. "Baby, stop crying. Please don't cry. Okay, here's the plan: you are going to sleep with the client, and if he wants his dick sucked, tell him that it's an extra five hundred dollars, deal?"

I didn't want to get hit again so I just agreed and commenced to go with the client.

"Okay, Jazzy."

"One more thing, Karmen...don't enjoy it too much. Your pussy belongs to me. You're my bitch, understood?"

"Your bitch?"

"My main girl, the only one that I truly love. I don't love Jenny or any of the other women."

I had felt like I was in a twilight zone because I was not only compared to other women, but now I was a co-worker of his. *Selling drugs, my ass,* I thought to myself. *How could I have been so stupid and naive to the possibility that the man I had fallen in love with was a pimp?*

"Karmen, get yourself together and get ready to leave with Mr. Henry."

"Okay."

"Once you are done with your evening, your car will be waiting outside for you, I want you to drive home and I will see you in the morning."

"Okay." The tears fell even harder because I didn't know what I had gotten myself into. I grabbed my coat and proceeded to go inside of the man's limo that was waiting outside of the club. Jazzy walked up to me as I was getting in the limo.

"Baby, I want you to know that I love you and things will change soon."

"Whatever."

He kissed me on the lips and I didn't kiss him back. I just gathered my things and got into the limo. I wondered what made him change me. I thought to myself, *this little exchange was not going to last always. I had a Master's degree to get.* Jazzy was going to have to put in a want ad because I was, indeed, no one's trick.

Krystol

"The Sex Exchange"

The limo driver took me to a hotel room. I was told to get a key at the front desk and head up to room 315. I still couldn't believe that I was about to sell my body and then cheat on my boyfriend due to my decision and his notion. I had on a long coat with the nurse's uniform because the client wanted me to wear it. I suddenly felt sick to my stomach as I walked up to the front desk.

"Welcome to the Hilton Hotel. How can I help you?"

"Yes, I would like a key to room 315, please. Someone is expecting me."

"Yes, ma'am. Mr. Jones is expecting you."

He gave me the key as he winked at me. I wanted to spit in his face. Apparently, Mr. Jones deals with a lot of different women on a regular basis. I got on the elevator to go on the third floor and there was a couple standing inside.

"Excuse me, can you please hit number three?"

"Sure, ma'am," the young woman beside the buttons said as she stood next to a young man. I got off of the elevator and walked down the hall, and there it was...room 315. I could hear slow music playing. I used my key and let myself in. The room was dark and there were candles lit. On the bed lay man in his early 30's with a body to die for. He had muscles galore, but this was still wrong, and I was scared as hell.

"Hey there, Karmen."

"Mr. Jones, let's get this done and over with."

"You don't want a glass of wine at least?"

"No." I started to pull off my jacket and let it fall to the floor.

"Karmen, you are exceptionally beautiful. If I hadn't known that you were Jazzy's bitch, I would have kept you to myself and married you." He started to jerk off while I was taking off all my clothes. His manhood rose at full attention. I just wanted to get this done and over with.

"Do you have the money?" I inquired.

"Yes. Look on the table and get it."

I looked on the table and grabbed the one thousand dollars. I put it in my coat pocket that lay on the floor. I, then, walked over to the bed and jerked him off with my hand. As he moaned from the hand job I gave him, a tear shed from my eye.

"Ugh...that's right, faster."

"Okay," I said as my voice started to tremble from my crying and nervousness. He couldn't see me because his eyes were closed, although candles were lit. Once I was done with the hand job, he grabbed the condom and put it on. I quickly climbed on top of him. He struggled to get all the way inside of me because I was dry, but he managed to enter me and I started to ride him.

"Karmen, this pussy is so good. Jazzy was right."

I thought to myself, *Jazzy was right?* I started to feel stupid because he had the idea of pimping me the whole time. How could I have been a fool? I started to ride faster, and Mr. Jones came within minutes.

"Oohh shit! Shit!" he moaned. "Damn girl, you are good."

"Okay, then. I'm going to go."

"Wait...why don't you take a shower and stay the night."

"Please. You say that as if you really give a fuck about me and you're my man or something."

"Well, now that I see you and I know that you are good at what you do, I'd like to have you with me full-time."

"No thanks. This was just a one-time thing for me."

"I'd doubt that; you love the money."

"My man, Jazzy, has money. I'm good."

"Yeah, you may be his main bitch, but you can be my wife."

"Main bitch?" I started yell at the man. "I'm his girlfriend!"

"Look, Karmen. He says that to all the girls that he has working for him."

When he said that, I could tell he was telling the truth because he had a serious look on his face. Tears were running down my face at this point.

"Karmen, come here." He was trying to console me, but I wanted no parts of him touching me.

"No, just leave me alone."

He dug in his pocket and took out a thousand dollars more. I was wondering what he was doing giving me more money.

"Here. I know that I paid for the night, but this is for you."

"I can't take this."

"Sweetheart, yes you can. I'm sorry that what I told you hurt you, but it's the truth."

"Thanks."

"Take my card in case you ever want to have lunch or talk. I am really interested in you, and not as a client."

I took his card and got dressed. I said my goodbyes to Mr. Jones and then I left. On the elevator, I just wanted to let it out and cry. I had to get myself together until I got outside. When I made it outside, sure enough, my car was there. The door was unlocked and my keys were on the passenger seat. On the drive home, I couldn't help but to talk to myself.

"Karmen what the fuck are you doing? I can't believe that you slept with someone for money."

I cried and cried until I pulled in front of my house. It was exactly 3:30 am. I took a quick shower and climbed into bed. In my mind, I was now a whore, a prostitute...a person whom I hadn't recognized. This couldn't have been my life, I wanted to go to school and make something of myself, not spread my legs so the next man could have a buck up. Things were going to change starting now. Jazzy was going to be like the class that I hated the most in school...history.

Krystol

"One Year Later"

"Jazzy, I'm tired of this lifestyle. I want out."

He punched me in the face twice and I fell on the floor of his apartment.

"Karmen, what the fuck do I keep telling you? You're my bitch, my main bitch, and you will get out when I'm done with you!"

I was still working for Jazzy. I have had about eighty more clients since the night I had my first one, and we moved to Atlanta. Jazzy made me tell my dad that I was going to college down there and I was able to call once a day so he wouldn't get worried. I haven't spoken to Meana in months. My social life is now non-existent because Jazzy said it was best for me to keep my head clear when I'm with clients.

"Jazzy, I'm just tired."

"Karmen do you want the day off and someone can take your spot just for a day?"

"No."

"Okay then."

"I'm tired of always asking you for money when I want to buy an outfit or anything."

"That's the way that I do business."

While he was talking, I began feeling nauseous. I ran into the bathroom and threw up. I had been getting sick for a while and I hoped that I wasn't pregnant again. I had two abortions since I started working for Jazzy. I had no recollection who the father was since I had a new client every night.

"Karmen, are you okay?"

While I was hovering over the toilet, I couldn't help but squint as I looked at Jazzy. I just knew that my eye was swollen shut from him hitting me.

"I don't know. I think I need to go to the hospital and get checked out."

"Okay. I'm going to give you some money so that you can go and I want you back here once your done."

"Okay."

I was glad that I was still able to drive my car around and not stand on the corners like some of the other coworkers did. I was tired of this business and there were only two ways out:

be killed or kill Jazzy. I had been planning, for some time now, how I would kill him. Jazzy gave me a small gun for protection when I was out late at night. I would use it to shoot and kill him.

Sitting in the emergency room, I couldn't wait to be seen by the doctor. I had a terrible cold that didn't go away, no matter how much medicine I took for it. I walked up to the receptionist in the emergency room.

"Yes, my name Karmen Watson and I've been nauseous and coughing up blood."

"Do you have a fever?"

"I'm not sure."

"Okay, let me put you in the system and take your temperature."

"Thank you, ma'am."

I went into one of the patients' rooms. I didn't know why I was coughing up blood.

"Ma'am, how long have you been getting abused?"

"Abused? Who said anything about being abused?"

"Well, you do have a black eye."

"Oh." I lowered my head down in shame. How did things get this far?

"Okay, now open up. I'm going to take your temperature."

The woman seemed so motherly. I wouldn't know what it would be like to have a mother because mine died while giving birth to me. My dad named me after her.

"Mmm hmm."

"What?"

"You have a fever of 102."

"Really?"

"Yes, ma'am. Are there any other symptoms that you are experiencing?"

"Yes. I have chills often and I cough up blood sometimes."

"Okay I'll let the doctor know. Sit back in the waiting room and I'll bump your name up on the list."

"Thank you."

"No problem. You know that you can leave this man, right?"

"Yes, ma'am. I'm doing that today."

I thought about the gun that I had in my glove compartment. I had planned on using it once I got back from the hospital. I was tired of the life that I had lived for a while now. I should have just kept walking when I saw him that day on Monroe Street in Delaware.

"Ma'am, could I have an HIV test today as well?"

"Yes. I can swab your mouth and the doctor will be able to tell you the results when you seem him today."

"Okay, thank you."

She swabbed my mouth, and although I knew that I was fine, I just had to make sure. Jazzy was the only one that I was having unprotected sex with. When the swab was done, I went back in the waiting room. It was very crowded with vending machines and people crying from being in pain. I leaned back to close my eyes when my cell phone went off. It was a text from Jazzy.

"Karmen what did the doctor say? Are you pregnant again?"

"I have a high fever and I'm waiting for the doctor now."

"Okay. I'll give you the next two days off, but keep me posted and get your ass back here once your done."

"Yes, daddy."

I couldn't wait to hurry back so that I could kill him when he was least expecting it. I was deep in thought about killing Jazzy when the nurse called me.

"Karmen Watson?"

"Yes, here."

"Please, come on back."

I got up and followed the nurse down the hall. When I walked into the room, the doctor was sitting in his chair.

"Hello Ms. Watson. I'm Dr. Benton, how are you?"

"Oh, doctor, I could be better."

"I see...well, we have your test results back. Now, Karmen, I want you to know that we have groups and people for you to talk to if you need them and medicine that will help you with the pain."

"The pain from what!"

I had started to cry because I didn't know what he was going to say. What in the world is wrong with me?

"Ms. Watson, your pregnancy test came back positive."

"Wow, okay. I guess that's good news."

"Yes, ma'am, it is...congratulations. Now, your test for herpes, Chlamydia, and syphilis were all negative."

"That's good."

"But your test for HIV was positive."

"What? Positive!!" I started to scream out loud and began to get frantic.

"Ma'am, we have someone here that you can talk to and you are able to get your medications for free through a program that's available."

"Oh my god! I'm dying."

"Ms. Watson, there are plenty of people who live long lives with HIV."

I started to fall to my knees as I hit the floor and I sobbed loudly. I couldn't believe that I had this terrible disease that there wasn't a cure for.

"Ms. Watson, is there anyone that can come get you?"

I stood there frozen, without saying a word, as I held my stomach.

"Ms. Watson?"

I was able to make eye contact, but I couldn't say a word. While I stood there frozen, my cell phone was going off and it was Jazzy calling.

"I'm fine...can I have my paperwork and some vitamins to take?"

"Sure, ma'am. Please make an appointment with a doctor so you can get a sonogram and get set up for a good doctor to deliver your baby."

"Okay, I will."

I took the medicine, prescriptions, and paperwork the doctor gave me and I was on my way. When I got back in my car, I cried uncontrollably. I cried until there were no more tears left to shed. I had no one to call, except one person.

"Hey baby."

"Daddy?"

"Yes, Karmen...what's wrong? Why are you crying? Is it school?"

"Dad, I'm not in school. I moved here to be with a man and he's been hurting me."

"Hurting you how?"

"Daddy, I'm pregnant."

"Pregnant?"

"Yes...pregnant, Dad. And I'm dying."

"Karmen being pregnant is not that big of a deal."

"No, Dad. I have HIV!" After I confessed to my dad, I cried even harder.

"Baby, are you sure?"

"Yes, Dad. I just got my test results back."

My dad got quiet and I could hear him starting to cry.

"Karmen get on the next flight here. Daddy will take care of you. I promise."

"Okay, Daddy. I love you," I said in between sobs as he hung the phone up.

Driving back to Jazzy's house, I was ready to kill him for real. Hell, he had already killed me; now it was his time to die. I pulled up to the house with the shotgun in my pocket. I barged open the door and heard silence.

"Jazzy, where the fuck are you?" I walked into the living room, but he wasn't there.

"Jazzy, you were right, I'm pregnant, but there is more."

The louder my voice got, the more silence I heard. When I walked into his bedroom, the smell of blood made me throw up instantly. Jazzy's body was in the floor next to his couch by his bed.

"Oh my God! Jazzy...Jazzy!!" I walked over to him to check his pulse, but there was nothing. I grabbed my phone to call the cops, but they had already busted in the door screaming.

"Get your hands up and back away from the body, ma'am!"

They scared the hell out of me. I had no choice but stand up. With my hands placed behind my back, a female cop searched me and found the shotgun that was in my pocket.

"Are you Karmen Watson?"

"Yes, ma'am but I didn't use that gun. I swear."

"Ms. Watson, you are under arrest for the murder of Jazon Smith."

"What?"

"We got a call that you shot this man."

"I just got here!"

"What were you doing with the gun in your pocket?"

"It was for protection."

"You have the right to remain silent. Anything you say can and will be held against you in the court of law. You have the right to an attorney. If you don't have an attorney, one can be appointed for you. Ma'am, do you understand your rights?"

I couldn't do anything but cry as they put me in the back of the police car. I was, then, taken to the police station, where I was fingerprinted. After I was fingerprinted, I was placed in a cell by myself until they took me the women's correctional institution. I couldn't believe that it came to this. Someone set me up for Jazzy's murder. The cops said that my prints were on the gun that killed him. As I was sitting in my cell, it dawned on me that the first night I had slept with that client, Jenny had bought me my car. I remember Jazzy telling me that. I don't remember having a shotgun. I remember Jazzy getting me a small handgun.

"That's it! Jenny set me up. She switched guns from my car!"

Here I was, pregnant, HIV positive, and locked up for a murder that I didn't commit...all because I decided to be Jazzy's bitch.

Krystol

www.ingramcontent.com/pod-product-compliance
Lightning Source LLC
Chambersburg PA
CBHW020142180626
46810CB00004B/1688